Totally Disgusting!

TOTALLY DISGUSTING!

by Bill Wallace

drawings by Leslie Morrill

Holiday House / New York

Library of Congress Cataloging-in-Publication Data

Wallace, Bill.
Totally disgusting! / by Bill Wallace : drawings by Leslie
Morrill. — 1st ed.
p.   cm.
Summary: Despite his uncourageous name, Mewkiss proves to
be a strong and brave kitten during a crisis in which his
mistress's life is threatened.
ISBN 0-8234-0873-6
1. Kittens—Juvenile fiction. [1. Cats—Fiction.]   I. Morrill.
Leslie H., ill.   II. Title.
PZ10.3.W162To   1991
[Fic]—dc20
90-47561   CIP   AC

To my friends at Grand and West in Chickasha, OK, and at Hubbard in Ramsey, NJ. Thanks for your help with the title.

Totally Disgusting!

Chapter 1

The smell of fear and the feel of my brothers and sisters crying woke me from a peaceful sleep.

"Mama? Mama!" they meowed. "We're hungry. Please feed us our breakfast. Mama? Mama, where are you?"

I rolled over on my tummy and stretched. It felt good to arch my back and stick my claws out. "What's wrong?" I said with a yawn. "Where's Mama?"

"We don't know," one of my brothers answered. "When we woke up she was gone. One of our brothers is missing, too."

Then we started to cry all at once and as loud as we could.

"Mama! Mama," we meowed. "Mama, please come back!!!"

"Hush, my children."

Mama's voice was far away but very stern and gruff. We got quiet.

We could feel the vibration of her paws walking on the cement floor. "Don't make so much racket," she scolded. "I'm here."

"Where have you been?" we mewed softly. "We were scared."

Mama stepped into the box of old rags that was our bed. "I told you that I was going to move you upstairs to my home with Mrs. Herst. She is my special person," Mama said. "She cares for me and I care for her. But she is quite old and doesn't see very well. If I had moved you earlier, she might have stepped on one of you. That is why I waited until your eyes opened and your ears could hear. I have taken your brother already. I can only carry you one at a time." She calmed us down by cleaning us with her tongue. "While I am away, there is no one here to protect you. So be very still."

One at a time, Mama carried my brothers and sisters upstairs. While she was gone, the rest of us stayed very quiet.

Finally, there were only three of us left—my sister, my brother, and me. Suddenly, we heard a strange scratching sound.

"Shhh," my brother said. "Remember, Mama told us not to make noise."

"It wasn't me," my sister said.

"I haven't moved," I told him.

The scratching sound came again. It was coming toward the box of rags where we lived. But when Mama came back to the basement, the sound stopped. She picked up my brother and scurried off.

As soon as she was gone, the scratching sound got louder. Then I smelled something that made the hair along my back stand straight up. My tail puffed out.

I didn't know what the smell was, but something down deep inside me made me scared and angry— both at the same time.

"Kittens," a sneaky, hushed voice snarled.

"Yes," another voice squeaked, "fat, juicy, kittens."

My claws sprang out. Every muscle tensed. I pushed against the side of the box and nestled down into the old rags.

"They'll make a good meal," the sneaky voice rasped. "They must be in that box."

I flattened my ears. Suddenly, my sister screamed. It was a loud, sharp scream. A scream of pain and terror. I turned to see what had happened, but there was nothing there except a scaly, long tail that disappeared over the top of the box.

Then there was nothing but silence.

"I'll take this one back to our rat hole," a muffled voice said from someplace outside the box. "You get the other one."

I couldn't see. There was nothing but the edge of the box. Still, I knew something was there. I could feel a presence—a sinister evil that drew closer and closer.

Crouched in the old rags, there was no way I could see what was about to attack me or where the attack was coming from. Trembling, I flipped over on my back at the edge of the box. I stuck all four legs up with my claws out.

I couldn't bear to look. My eyes scrunched shut. I held my breath. Waited.

There was the sound of breathing. Then, sniffing. The evil thing was trying to find me by my smell. I heard claws scratching against the side of my box and felt hot breath touch my face and whiskers.

I lashed out with my claws. I used my front paws to scratch at the darkness. I kicked with my hind feet.

The first claw of my right paw touched something. I lashed out again.

There was a shrill squeak that shook the air in tiny waves. "Ouch! My nose . . ." Then the raspy, evil smell that said, "I'll show you. I'll . . ." The scent drew closer, but I never heard the rest of the threat.

KERWHOMP!!!

Something big and heavy and hard glanced against the side of my box. It sent it sliding across the floor. My eyes flashed open. The rat squealed. A loud, shrill squeal of pain. The smell of its fear faded as it flew across the room, away from me.

"Stinking rat." A man's scent filled the air.

I could hear small, skinny feet scurrying toward the thing they'd called a rat hole, where the other "rat" had taken my sister. Then, there was a loud, metal CLUNK.

"No, you don't," the man growled. "You're not sneaking through that hole. I've got you this time."

"Help! Help," the rat squeaked.

I could feel the man stomping at the floor. I could sense the rat scurrying and running here and there. Then another smell came to my nose. It was the odor of my mama's fear and anger.

"My babies! My babies," she cried.

She leaped into the box. After one quick sniff of me, to make sure I was all right, she leaped out again. I tried to see where she had gone, but the edge of the box was too high.

"Thatagirl," the man urged. "Get him. Good cat . . ."

The man kept stomping his big foot. Mama screamed her rage. The rat threatened, then cried and ran.

It was a terrible fight. It raged to the far side of the basement, back toward me, then away again. Boxes tumbled. Mama snarled and leaped. The rat hissed and snapped.

Finally, it was over.

"Good girl," the man said. "You're a good cat. That stinking rat won't be bothering us anymore, will he, girl?"

Mama rushed to me. I was still on my back. My claws were still out. My heart pounded in my ears harder than I thought was possible.

Mama licked me with her tongue. "You're all right," she told me with a soft caress. "I'm so glad you're safe. Lie here quietly. I'll be right back."

She rushed to the hole where the other rat had taken my sister. "Oh, my poor baby," I heard her moan in a soft, sad tone. "My poor, poor baby."

I had rolled to my side in the soft rags. I lay very still, panting and trying to stop my shaking.

"No wonder you fought so hard." The sound of the man's voice boomed above me. It was very close and very loud.

I flipped to my back and stuck my claws out again.

"No wonder you fought so hard," he repeated. "You've got a baby in here. I bet that stinking rat was after your kitten."

Mama came back and jumped into the box beside me. "Be calm, my baby," she soothed. "The man is nice. Don't use your claws. He means you no harm."

I saw the man lean close. His huge paw picked me up. Another paw petted my head and smoothed down my fur. Then the man put me back in my bed.

Mama cleaned me. She calmed me with her tongue and her soft words as she kept assuring me I was safe.

"You take care of your baby," the man said from the far side of the basement. "I'll take this stinking rat to the trash."

"My sister . . ." I pleaded. "Mama, what happened to my sister?"

Mama's tongue was gentle against my closed eyes. "She's gone, I'm afraid. The hole was too small for me to enter, but I could smell death. Your sister is gone." She picked me up in her mouth. "I must take you to your brothers and sisters," she said. "You'll be safe with them and Mrs. Herst."

At the doorway of the basement, we paused. With

me dangling from her mouth, Mama turned to look back.

She said nothing, but I could almost feel what she was thinking. The rats would pay for the death of my sister. Mama would be back.

Chapter 2

We all missed our sister terribly.

Mama told us that feeling sorry for her or feeling sorry for ourselves wouldn't help. There was nothing we could do to bring her back. The only thing we could hope for would be that someday we'd grow up to be big and strong and brave—and kill rats.

Mama's words helped. That night, I felt brave and strong. But in the middle of the night, I had a frightful dream. In the dark, I could feel a ratty, evil presence. I could hear the scratching of tiny claws coming closer and closer.

My claws sprang out. I struck at the blackness.

"Ouch," my brother shrieked.

His voice woke me from my sleep. "He scratched me, Mama."

Mama came quickly. I was panting. My heart pounded in my ears and my tail fluffed out big and round.

"It was the rat," I panted. "He was after me, Mama."

Mama licked my ears with her tongue. "It was only a dream. Just a bad dream."

Mama curled up close to me. She gave me some milk. Finally my heart stopped pounding so loudly. My tail smoothed down and I went to sleep.

The horrible dreams tormented my sleep almost every night. But in two weeks, they seemed to fade away. Still I worried that they might return.

A few weeks later, while we were having lunch, Mama told us the story of how we cats would find our special person.

"The first night you spend with your people family is when you'll meet your special person," she told us.

"You will know your special person by the light in his eyes and the love in his hands when he picks you up and holds you for the first time. You will know in your heart that this one is yours.

"This human is also the one who will give you

your name. The way a cat is given his or her name
is a very unique ritual, indeed.

"No matter who else may speak to you, no matter
what they may say, you will not listen. But the moment your special person picks you up, you must
hear every word.

"You must watch his eyes. From the moment
your eyes meet, the first name he says will be yours
for *always*. Your name can never be stolen or taken
away. Your name can never be changed. Your name
is your name—forever."

When Mama finished with her story, I felt myself
begin to purr.

"I hope my special person gives me a brave
name," I mused. "I hope I get a strong name, like
Fearless or Ratkiller. I hope my name is so strong
and brave that I'm never afraid of anything—not
ever again!"

When we finished eating and our tummies were
full, Mama also told us that people would be coming
soon to look at us and take us to live with them.

We didn't want to go. We didn't want to leave our
mama. But she just laughed and told us that that is
what cats are supposed to do. Living with people is
how cats are supposed to live, and now that we were
eight weeks old, we could no longer be babies and
stay at home with her.

It was very hard for me to get to sleep that night. I kept thinking about the dreams. What would it be like to wake up and not have Mama curled up next to me?

I hoped my people would be nice. I hoped they would be warm and friendly and feed me good food and pet me. And I hoped my special person would give me a good, strong, brave name, so I wouldn't be scared or have bad dreams.

Chapter 3

The next morning, a little boy and his father came from just down the street and took my brother. As the rest of us waited for our people to come, we talked about how wonderful it would be if we could all stay in the same neighborhood. That way, when our people let us out at night to prowl, we could see each other.

Then a woman came and took my sister to a strange world called Queens.

Each day my excitement grew and grew as, one by one, my six brothers and sisters were chosen by their people. Finally, only my sister and I were left. I felt a little scared. What if no one wanted me? What if I wasn't picked?

I might end up like my father—just an old alley

cat, roaming the streets of New York on my own. What if I didn't have a special person? What if I didn't have a name? It would be terrible not to have a name!

Then it happened.

The man seemed young, but he had white hair. He was jolly and nice. He smelled clean and happy. He picked my sister up and looked at her. Then he picked me up, and smiled.

"I'll take this one," he told Mrs. Herst.

(I liked the man. But I could tell he was not my special person.)

"Good choice," Mrs. Herst said. "He's a good, healthy kitten. Is he yours or a present?"

"A present," the man answered.

"I hope he'll have a good home."

The man smiled. "I think so. He's going to New Berlin. It's over in the center of the state. Near Norwich. He is going to be a birthday present for my daughter. I have twins—one boy, one girl. My son's been wanting a dog. The girl, well . . . this kitten is for her."

The man cradled me in his arm. I leaned to the side so I could see my mama and my sister. "Good-bye."

Mama smiled. "Good-bye. Be good to your special person." She meowed softly.

Outside the apartment, Mrs. Herst told the man that since he had such a long drive, he might need a box to carry me in.

"There're a few spare boxes in the basement," she said.

I froze. Every muscle in my body went stiff.

"Not the basement!" My insides screamed, but I didn't make a sound. "Please don't take me to the basement. The rats live in the basement!"

I stayed very still as we went down the stairs. When we finally got to the first floor, the man who was carrying me followed Mrs. Herst through the long hallway. When she opened the door to the basement, my heart stopped beating. The smell of rat came to my nose. But I was so scared, my whiskers didn't even twitch.

"Wait here," she told the man. "I'll be right back."

I was so thankful that we didn't go down there, I almost fainted. Mrs. Herst came back and handed the man a box. At the front door, we stopped and they put me in it. It was dark when they shut the lid, but I wasn't scared. Then we got in a car and drove and drove and drove.

A first, there was a whole lot of noise. We stopped and started and stopped and started.

A few times, I stretched and tried to wiggle my

head so I could see out the top of the box. Only the way they had it folded, I couldn't get it open. Once, I did get my head through the crack, but as soon as I did, the man shoved me back down.

We drove for a long, long time. Finally, the car stopped and the man turned it off. He picked up my box, and we went inside a house. I could tell because of the way the smell changed from the car to the fresh, clean outside, then to the different smell of a house.

I could smell that the house was old. Very old. But it was clean and warm and friendly. I could hear other people's voices. A soft, woman's voice said, "Hi, honey, glad you're home. Did you get the kitten?"

She opened the top of my box, and I blinked as I looked up. Our eyes met—but the woman was not my special person. She had a pretty smile and a nice, soft voice. But she wasn't mine.

"Oh, he's darling," she exclaimed, closing up my box again. "You need to go next door and get the puppy. James called about thirty minutes ago. He said that dog's been crying and howling so much that our kids are bound to hear him. I've almost got the cake finished."

I heard the man leave.

I could smell a cake baking in the oven. I knew what cake was because Mrs. Herst used to make them. Sometimes, she would let us eat the leftovers after her company was gone. I *loved* cake, especially the sweet top part of it.

I sure hoped she would let me have some of it. I heard a door open and the man's voice again.

"Where should I put the puppy?"

"How about the garage?" the woman answered.

He and the woman talked for a moment, then I heard a door open again.

"Timmy! Jessica!" The woman called in a loud voice. "You two stay away from that cellar. There could be spiders or snakes or hard-telling-what in there. Come in and get cleaned up for supper." Then she said softly to the man: "Put the cat's box next to the dog's. Maybe if they're close enough so the puppy can hear the cat, he won't start howling."

My box bounced around some, and when it set down again, I could smell the odor of cars and gasoline and oil. I didn't like the smell. I heard something scratching.

I had to see what was going on. With all my strength, I stood up and pushed my head against the top of the box.

Suddenly, the crack at the top opened enough for

me to stick my head out. I could see a box next to my box. It wiggled some. From inside, there was a soft, whimpering sound.

"I'm so scared. Why won't they let me out of this box? I just know my people are going to be mean to me. I want out. I want my mama. I'm scared . . ."

"Who's there?" I asked.

I heard a growl. Then the box next to mine got real still.

I tried to get my paws through the crack where my neck was. There wasn't enough room. In fact, the crack was so tight, my neck was starting to hurt. It was hard to breathe, too.

I decided to pull my head back into the box. Only, when I tried to, I got stuck. I jerked and jumped and twisted and turned. No matter what I did, my head wouldn't come loose. My eyes started to bug out. I could hardly catch my breath.

Lifting my hind feet off the bottom, I squirmed and flopped from side to side.

I was really STUCK!

I couldn't get back in the box. I couldn't get out of the box. I could hardly breathe. I just knew I was going to die. I was stuck there—hung by the neck.

It was all over and I hadn't even met my special person. I didn't even have a brave name—and I would probably die before I ever did.

Chapter 4

It was the man who saved me. My eyes were so big from lack of air, I thought they were going to pop clear out of my head. Just seconds before I passed out and died, he came running into the garage.

When he saw my head, he grabbed the lid of the box and pried it loose. Then he stuffed me back down.

"Dumb cat," he mumbled. He picked up my box, and we went into the house.

From the other room, I could hear the woman's voice. "And this one's for you, Timmy."

I could hear paper rattling. I could hear voices talking and laughter. "Oh, boy!" the boy's voice said. "Three new Nintendo games."

And a higher, lighter voice said, "Oh, Mama, a new doll. Thank you."

"Your father has something for you, too," the woman said.

Suddenly, something shook my box. It bounced me around. I banged against the side a couple of times. My eyes crossed.

"What is it, Daddy?"

"Careful, Jessica," the man said. I could feel other hands on my box as I was set down on the floor and light flooded in. I had to close my eyes because it was so bright. Hands wrapped around me and lifted me from my box.

The hands were soft and gentle, but they trembled with excitement. "Oh, Daddy!!!" the voice yelped. "Oh, Daddy . . . thank you! What a beautiful kitty."

I blinked. My eyes finally got used to the light and I could see.

It was a girl. For the first time, I looked into her eyes. And just as Mama had told me—I knew that *this* was my special person.

My breath caught in my throat. I felt warm all over. I waited—for the next thing she said as she looked at me would be my name.

Only, she didn't say anything.

Instead, she turned to look at a little boy opening another box beside us. "Oh, Daddy," the boy squealed, "a dog! A real, live dog. Oh, Daddy! I love him! I've always wanted a dog. He's great, Dad!!!"

My whiskers twitched. A dog? I thought to myself. That's what was wiggling and whining in the box next to me? Dogs are horrible. Who'd want a yucky dog?

I watched my girl's eyes. She kept looking at her brother and that icky dog. From inside the box, the dog could sense the boy's excitement. He looked up at him and started barking.

It was more like a squeak, really. But he barked and barked.

The boy laughed. "He's barking at us. You're a real barker." He giggled. Then he looked at his daddy. "He's barking at us," the boy repeated.

His eyes twinkled and got real big. "I know what," he said with a smile. He swooped the puppy up in his arms and held him out at arm's length. "I'm going to call you Barkus."

The man and woman laughed. "That's a neat name for a dog," they agreed. "Barkus. That's cute."

They all laughed again—even my girl.

I held my breath when she turned her face back toward me. She petted me. She looked at my eyes. Only, she didn't say anything. Instead, she turned to the man and woman.

"Look at me," I meowed. "Look at my eyes and give me a good name."

When I meowed the second time, my girl giggled. "My kitty said 'mew.'" She hugged me so tight, I couldn't move. When she did, my whiskers crunched against her cheek.

That made her laugh. "My kitty gave me a kiss! He said mew, then he gave me a kiss."

Suddenly, she stopped laughing and got very quiet.

"Barkus is a neat name for a dog," she said. "I know what I'm going to name my kitty . . ."

I trembled with excitement. I knew that any second our eyes would meet and I would have my name.

". . . Timmy named his dog Barkus, because he barks at us. My kitty said mew and gave me a kiss. I'm going to call him . . ."

At long last our eyes met! The next word would be my name!

". . . MEWKISS."

Chapter 5

Mewkiss?

How totally disgusting!

I said the name over and over to myself. When I said it slowly, Mew kiss, Mew kiss, it sounded like the words "Mew" and "Kiss" put together. But if I said it fast: Mewkiss. Mewkiss, mewkiss . . .

It sounded like the stuff Mrs. Herst complained about that time she had a cold. It sounded like mucus. You know—the yucky, slimy, crud people cough up when they have a cold.

What a horrible name.

Mama had told us that it was better to have a name that didn't make sense, than to have no name at all. But Mewkiss???

*   *   *

I wanted to die. My first night with my people family was supposed to be wonderful, but I just wanted to curl up in a corner and be left alone.

My girl was named Jessica. She petted me and rubbed me. Every time her cheek touched my whiskers, she'd giggle and squeal, "he kissed me again . . ."

Finally, I got loose from her and went to explore.

She *was* my "special person" but after the name she'd stuck me with, I didn't care. I wanted to get away from her.

That night, they locked me in the kitchen. It really wasn't all that bad. They made a bed for me out of an old carpet. They put a box with litter in it near the corner so I could go to the bathroom if I needed to. Then they turned the light out.

I decided that maybe a good night's sleep would make me feel better.

But as soon as the lights went out, Barkus started howling from his spot in the garage.

"I'm lonely," he yapped. "I want my boy, Timmy. I want my mama. I'm scared of the dark. I want in the house. I'm scared. . . ."

The daddy walked through my kitchen a couple of times and tried to get him quiet. Only, the dumb dog wouldn't shut up. Finally, the man put him in the kitchen with me.

That didn't help either. He just kept yowling and scratching the back of the kitchen door.

The second night I was with my people family, they decided that maybe the puppy would be quiet if they put us together in a small place where the puppy would be close to me. Either a big box, or . . .

. . . the bathtub.

They put a towel down in the bottom of the tub and stuck me in there with that smelly mutt.

He must have carried on for well over an hour. No matter how I tried to get him to be quiet, he kept on howling and whining. I told him things would be all right. I told him that I was lonely, too. "I miss my mama and brothers and sisters every bit as much as you do," I said. Only, he didn't listen.

Finally, our people came in. The first time, the mama petted him and talked real soft. Barkus got quiet, but as soon as she turned the light off and left, he started howling again.

In a few minutes, the daddy came in. He wasn't

as nice and soft as the mama. He made a mean face.

"Hush up and go to sleep!" he shouted, shaking his finger at Barkus.

Barkus whimpered very softly and lay his head down on the towel. But as soon as the light went out, his whimpering got louder and louder. In no time at all, he was yowling again.

When the daddy came back a second time, he had a rolled-up newspaper in his hand. He didn't hit Barkus, but he banged the paper against the side of the bathtub. It made an awful sound. Barkus jumped back and tucked in his stub tail.

"Hush up, *right now!*" the daddy roared. His voice was so mean and loud it shook the glass doors at the side of our bathtub. "One more peep and you can both spend the night outside in the storm cellar. I don't care how cold it is down there."

He wheeled around and hit the switch on the wall with his newspaper. It made a loud popping sound and things got dark. Then he slammed the door and stormed off down the hall.

When the daddy said "storm cellar" my heart pounded in my ears. I felt the chills race up my back—clean from the tip of my tail to my pointy ears. My tail began to fluff. I shook all over.

"Not the storm cellar," I called after him. "A storm cellar is like a basement and it probably has rats!"

Only the daddy didn't hear me. Or, if he did hear, he didn't understand.

When the daddy left, Barkus was quiet for a long time. I couldn't stop trembling. The thought of a cellar—a basement—scared me.

Then the dumb dog started that darned whimpering again.

"I don't want him to throw me in the cellar," he sniffed. "What's a cellar?"

"It's like a basement. I was born in a basement. It's a cold, dark, frightening place. And if you keep making noise and get us thrown down there . . . well . . . you'll be sorry. Now hush!"

"I'm scared of the dark," Barkus moaned. "I want the light on. I want my mama. I want . . ."

I stood up, arching my back.

"Oh, shut up!"

Barkus's pointed ears perked up.

"Huh?"

"Shut up!" I hissed, moving closer to him. "If you keep howling and whining, he *will* throw us in the cellar. Rats live in cellars and basements. Rats eat kittens and puppies. Now, be quiet!"

He flopped down so hard, I almost scooted off my edge of the towel. When he hit, it made kind of a WHOOPF sound. Finally, he fell asleep.

Chapter 6

I *loved* my Jessica. We played and cuddled. I purred and rubbed against her, and she stroked my fur and scratched behind my ears and under my chin. We played chase the string.

I liked that game. I would pretend the string was a mouse or a nasty rat. I'd stalk it and creep up on it. Then, fast as a streak of lightning, I'd pounce. When I caught the end, it made me feel quick and strong and brave, the way cats are supposed to be.

Sometimes, we didn't even play. We just sat and watched TV or Jessica read a book. Lots of times she would read part of her book to me. I enjoyed listening to her voice and the words. Mostly, though, she read to herself.

*   *   *

In the mornings, the mama would come and open the door to the bathroom. She would pick up Barkus in one hand and me in the other. As soon as we got downstairs to the kitchen, she would put Barkus out the back door.

HE GOT TO GO OUTSIDE!

Me—well, as soon as the mama closed the door, she'd set me down in the cat box. It was full of kitty litter. It was kind of powdery and it felt gritty on my paws.

I usually needed to go to the bathroom, after being cooped up all night in the bathtub with Barkus. But, for the life of me, I couldn't understand why she wouldn't let me go outside.

After a while, she would go to the back door to call Barkus. Once, I tried to sneak out while she held the door open for him. The mama just shoved me back with her foot. I didn't even get a good smell of the outdoors, much less a good look at it.

The next morning, I tried to sneak through the door when the mama called Barkus in for breakfast. But again, she was too quick for me and shoved me back with her foot.

Finally, one Sunday afternoon, my Jessica took me outside!

It was just as wonderful as I'd hoped—even more so, in fact. There were smells everywhere. The grass felt soft and light beneath my feet. The little grains of dirt stuck to my paws. Wind blew the leaves of the trees. Wind touched my fur and made it tingle.

I *loved* the outdoors.

My Jessica followed me everywhere. I ran around in the grass for a moment. Jessica giggled when I lay down and rubbed against it and rolled over.

Then I spotted some tall plants up near the house. I went to investigate. The smell of other cats was there. They had marked these bushes with their scent as part of their territory. I rubbed against some of the bushes, leaving my own scent.

Now all the other cats would know that this house was mine. They would realize that there was a cat who lived here.

I went clear around the house, exploring the bushes as Jessica followed. She kept telling me that I was safe and that I shouldn't be scared.

I guess she figured I was nervous or something. I really wasn't—I was just excited about getting to look around in this huge, wonderful outdoors place. When we made our circle and came back to the place where I had started marking my territory, my Jessica got tired of following me and went to sit in the middle of the yard.

I explored more things, and finally, I went to thank her for bringing me out.

I nestled into her lap, and she cuddled me close. My purr started rumbling inside when she petted me and smoothed my fur down. Then she scratched me behind my ears.

It felt good to be in her arms. Above us, the sun felt warm. As I began to relax, my eyes got real heavy.

I lay my head on my paws. A nap would be very, very nice.

My eyes had barely closed when I heard a loud BOOM! Startled, I looked around.

Timmy and Barkus came flying through the back door. They charged across the yard toward us. Timmy was in front and Barkus was yapping, right at his heels.

Jessica's muscles tensed as she sat up. I felt tight and nervous, too, as they charged straight at us.

A few feet away, Timmy dropped to the ground. He slid across the grass on his leg and one hip. His big tennis shoe crashed against Jessica's knee.

"Safe," he yelled. "He was safe. Home run! Timmy Chapin wins the game for the home team."

Then he jumped to his feet and started strutting around with his hands clasped above his head. My ears twitched and my whiskers wiggled. People sure were strange, sometimes.

Jessica rubbed her knee. "That hurt," she complained. "Why do you always have to be such a nerd?"

She didn't have long to rub her knee or fuss at Timmy, though. Right then, Barkus leaped in. He jumped, trying to lick her face. His whole back end wiggled—almost out of control—as he wagged his little, stub tail. Jessica shoved him away, only he charged right back.

This time, she sent him spinning across the yard. It didn't bother Barkus. He rolled a couple of times, scampered to his feet, and came racing back to try and lick her again. She laughed at the crazy way he acted and the silly way his rear end wiggled back and forth.

The more she laughed, the more excited Barkus got. He started racing round and round her. Once, he slammed into me and almost knocked me off my feet.

Barkus was too wild and crazy for me. I got up, flipped my tail, and moved away.

"Let's play catch," Timmy said, shaking Jessica's shoulder. "Maybe we can teach Barkus to chase the ball. Come on!"

He had a white ball in his hand. He shoved it under her nose and shook her shoulder some more. Jessica got to her feet. They stood a little ways apart and started tossing the ball.

Dumb old Barkus didn't know what he was supposed to do. He ran back and forth, jumping against
Jessica's leg, then against Timmy's, trying to get
them to pet him. It was like he didn't even see the
ball they were trying to get him to chase. Even
when Timmy jiggled it under his nose and rolled it
to Jessica, Barkus didn't know what he was supposed to do.

Suddenly, he spotted me. His pointy ears went
straight up. His brown eyes got real big, and he got
that sneaky look on his silly face.

In a flash, his short, stubby, little legs brought
him charging toward me.

I couldn't believe how quickly he was coming. It
was hard to understand how those little, short legs
could bring him racing across the yard *so* fast.

I held my breath and waited.

When Barkus was only inches away, I jumped. I
went straight up in the air as Barkus charged un-
derneath me. Then I lit gently on the ground behind him.

He stopped a few feet away. His ears went up and
he cocked his head to the side—as if asking: "Where
did he go? Where did he go?"

Finally, he turned around. I smiled at him. Then,
teasing, I flipped my tail.

Instantly, he spun around and charged for me again.

The same trick worked a second time. But, now, Barkus had it figured out. This time, when he came racing toward me, expecting me to leap over him, I dodged to the side.

He tried to stop and turn. Only, he was going too fast, and his leg gave way. He went sliding into the dirt on the side of his head.

Barkus got up and shook himself. Wiggling his lip, he tried to get the grass and dirt out of the corner of his mouth.

"Dogs sure are clumsy," I sneered.

That little, stub tail of his started wagging. "You'll think clumsy," he laughed. "Just wait till I get hold of you."

We ran all over the yard. I managed to stay just a step or two ahead of him. When he'd get too close, I'd sidestep or double back. A couple of times, he tried to turn too sharply and went tumbling, head over stub tail. But he always got up and came racing after me again.

Timmy and my Jessica laughed and laughed at us.

Near the side of the yard, I saw a tall mound of dirt. There was a pile of bricks sticking up from one end of it.

If I dodged just as Barkus was coming over that mound, I bet he'd really take a good tumble going downhill.

Slowing, I let him get close enough so he could almost grab my tail. Then, just as I ran over the mound, I jumped sideways and stopped on top of the square pile of bricks. I felt the wind as Barkus went racing past.

Sure enough, when he tried to stop and turn, his legs went KERR-PLOP. He did about four somersaults before he landed on his back at the bottom of the hill.

Startled and surprised, he got up and shook himself.

"Up here, dummy," I taunted.

He turned and started toward me. He shook himself again and bounced up and down on his front legs. I sort of strutted around the top of the bricks, flipping my tail at Barkus.

He had just started up the hill toward me when a smell came to my nose. I sniffed again. The smell came from a hole in the middle of the bricks. It was a hole that went straight down into an opening beneath the mound of dirt.

Suddenly, my claws sprang out. My tail fluffed up, almost as big around as my body. The hair rushed to a sharp peak down the center of my back.

It all happened so fast, I didn't even know what was wrong.

"What is it?" Barkus asked from behind me. He must have sensed my fear. His voice was serious and he was no longer snapping at my tail.

My eyes got big as I glared at the hole.

"What's wrong?" Barkus repeated.

The air caught in my throat. My chest was so tight I could hardly breathe. The word I answered him with almost choked me.

"RATS!"

Chapter 7

What happened next, I'm not sure. One minute, I was looking down into the dark hole in the center of the pile of bricks. The next, I found myself clinging to the screen door at the back of the Chapins' house.

How I got there, I'm still not sure.

I meowed at the top of my lungs, begging someone to let me in. Only nobody understood.

I guess my Jessica thought I was still playing with Barkus or just plain acting silly. She didn't come to comfort or protect me. She and Timmy laughed and kept tossing the ball. Barkus came.

I looked down and saw him standing there, below me. He smiled and wagged his stub tail. His smile wasn't a silly one—he wasn't making fun of me for running away. Instead, I could tell that he was wor-

ried about me and smiled because he thought it
would help me relax.

"It's an old smell," he told me. "The animals that
left it were there a long, long time ago."

Slowly, I backed my way down the screen door.
"Are you sure?"

Barkus's smile was gentle. He nodded. "There's
been lots of rain and wind since the last smell was
left. I bet it's been months."

"But . . . but . . ." I stammered.

"It's all right. It's safe." He licked my ear a couple
of times. "Come on. I'll go with you. You'll be okay."

Barkus led the way across the yard. I followed a
few steps behind. Every now and then, I would stop
and sniff the air. My paws trembled with each step.
My muscles were tight—ready to run at the slight-
est sound or movement from the pile of bricks.

It took a lot of patience for Barkus to get me back
to that mound of dirt. On one side of the mound was
a metal door. It was silvery colored and slick. Barkus
trotted right past it. I made a wide arc around it. At
the pile of bricks on the far side of the mound, he
stopped. Then, smiling back at me, he wagged his
tail.

"Come on and smell for yourself. There's nothing
here. It's a real, real old smell."

Barkus was right. The smell was old. The rats were not here and hadn't been for a long time.

I checked all around the mound of dirt. It was the cellar that the daddy had threatened to put us in the first night we came to live with the Chapins. The pile of bricks was an air hole. At one time, there had been a fire in it. But that was long, long, ago. I guess when there had been a fire, it let the smoke out. When there hadn't been a fire, it let fresh air into the cellar.

I was glad Barkus had made me go back and sniff at it again. Now, at least, I knew there really were no rats around. I wasn't nearly as scared anymore.

Still, my insides felt all tight and jumpy.

So, I guess it was my fault we got thrown out of the bathtub.

I really felt guilty about it, too. I mean, Barkus had been specially nice to me. He was patient and gentle when he took me back to show me that there weren't any rats. Then, instead of being nice back to him, I got us thrown out. It really wasn't my fault, though.

That night I had a dream. It was a dream about the rats and my sister and me. And in the darkness I felt that evil presence coming for me and I lashed out.

When I awoke, there was no rat. My mother wasn't there to comfort me or make me feel safe. There was only Barkus.

He was huddled at the far side of the tub. He yapped and whined at the top of his voice. I trembled and shook myself awake. He was rubbing at a deep scratch above his eye.

We were lucky that my claw hadn't put his eye out.

The daddy came in to see why Barkus was crying. He was mad that I'd scratched Barkus and said some bad things to me. Then he left us alone and went back to sleep.

The next day, Barkus and I stayed in the garage while our family was away at work and school. I didn't like the garage because it smelled bad. But that night, we got to come in the house and play with our family, and at bedtime, the mama put us in our bathtub.

The dream came again.

This time I didn't scratch Barkus. I did scare him, though. When I woke up, he was whining at the far side of the tub. The daddy stormed in and took us to the garage.

That's where we stayed for the next week. Barkus didn't like the smell of the garage any more than I did. At night, he would cry and beg the Chapins to let us come back inside. It was cold and lonely. Each night seemed to get just a little colder than the night before.

The mama and the daddy didn't like Barkus's whining and crying every night. So they had some men come and build a fence around the yard and build a "dog" house for us to sleep in.

Outside was wonderful during the day. At night, it was a different matter. There were all sorts of strange sounds and strange smells that floated on the night air.

Barkus knew many of the smells. He had been born in a kennel not far from here. He knew the smell of skunk, opossum, deer, turkey, and squirrel. He taught me to tell the difference between them, and since he knew so much about the animals, neither one of us was afraid.

He told me that skunks and opossum weren't very nice, but they were scared to death of people and probably wouldn't come this close to a house—especially now that there was a fence. He said that the deer and turkey were even more scared of people than the other animals—besides, they were nice and never tried to hurt anybody or anything.

Since Barkus knew the smells, they didn't scare him. The sounds—the noises that went THUMP in the night—made him *very* nervous.

If there was a "scrape" or a "scratch" or "bump," he'd sit straight up in our house. His pointy ears would almost bump the roof.

"What's that?" he'd gasp. "Did you hear it? What was it?"

One night, a little limb fell off a tree and landed on the roof. Barkus leaped to his feet. He stood with his flat nose and his pointy ears aimed at the opening to our house and started barking. He barked and barked and barked until it gave me such a headache I thought my whiskers were going to fall off. I finally went outside, picked the stick up in my mouth, and brought it back in so he'd shut up.

It made me feel silly. I mean—I've seen dogs running around with a stick in their mouth—but never a cat. Still, it was the only way to get him quiet so I could sleep.

Chapter 8

For the next two weeks, things stayed pretty quiet. Our family let us come in at night so Timmy and Jessica could play with us. I liked listening to my Jessica read. On weekends, the children stayed home from school, so we played in the backyard. I loved to be with my Jessica.

During the weekdays, when everyone was away, there wasn't much for Barkus to do. Since the new fence was put up, he couldn't get out and explore. He was stuck in the yard.

The fence was no problem for me. I could hop over it or squeeze through the crack beside the gate. And even though I hated to leave Barkus all alone, I had to explore. Exploring is simply something we cats *have* to do.

I found all sorts of interesting things. Behind our house were mostly hills and woods. There were skunks and opossum who lived there, but remembering what Barkus had told me about them, I would go in the other direction whenever I smelled one. I met some squirrels once. They didn't want to talk or play, though. They told me that I would chase them and be mean to them. I promised I wouldn't. They said that maybe I wouldn't, now. But when I got grown up, I probably would.

In front of our house was a big, wide road. Cars whizzed up and down it. I stayed away from that, too. I remembered what my mama had told me about cars, when I lived in the city.

Next door in a house made of brown stone I discovered a big, old cat. His name was Allergies.

He was kind of sickly most of the time, always sneezing and coughing. Allergies told me that he was a Christmas present for a boy named Chuck. Only, he knew the first night that Chuck wasn't his special person. Chuck's mama was. When she picked him up, she was telling her husband that a cat was all she needed to really stir up her . . . then their eyes met, and she said . . . "Allergies."

"Like a good cat," Allergies sniffled, "I've tried hard to live up to my name."

I had a funny feeling when I was around Allergies. There was something about him that made me feel he was very smart—very wise. Still, Allergies wasn't much fun to play with. He was old and cranky. Besides, I was always a little afraid that I might catch something from him.

Beyond his house was another road, with even more cars racing up and down it. So I did a lot of my exploring in the woods.

Most of my trips were short ones. I hated to leave Barkus all alone. Once I'd gotten used to his "puppy smell," he really wasn't that bad. In fact, next to my Jessica, Barkus was my best friend in the whole world.

One night, a sound as faint and light as a butterfly's tongue touching the petals of a flower woke me from my sleep.

I yawned and rubbed my eyes with the back of my paw. I held my breath, listening to the gentle sound that seemed to caress the roof of our house.

Barkus must have heard the sound a few seconds after I did. He didn't yawn and blink his eyes, though. Instead, his brown eyes flashed open and he sprang to his feet. He yanked his head from side to side, searching for what was making the noise.

Then, he cowed down and kind of scrunched into the far corner of our house.

"What is it?" he whined. "What's making that terrible noise?"

I cocked my head to the side. "It's not a terrible noise," I told him. "It's soft and beautiful. Just listen."

Barkus frowned. His ears went up, listening. Then they folded down as if to protect his head. "It's not beautiful. It's a strange noise. I don't like strange noises."

My whiskers wiggled.

"Anything that soft and gentle can't hurt us."

"I don't like it," he pouted. "Go see what it is. Please."

"You big baby," I teased. "I've never seen anybody so scared of a little noise."

I stretched when I got to my feet. I stuck out my claws and kneaded the towels. Then I walked to the opening. The sound was louder here. It not only touched the roof of our house, but the green blades of grass and the brown dirt and the trees. The sound was all around.

I stuck my head out the doorway. It was like the air around our house had turned white. The white drifted down from the sky. It floated and fell as gently as the sound I had heard. The white specks were glistening—an almost silver-white instead of simply white. I leaned out farther, and one of the little specks touched my whiskers.

Quickly, I yanked my head back inside.

"What is it?" Barkus asked from behind me. "What's out there?"

"I don't know."

Again, I stuck my head through the opening. I crinkled my nose up so I could see the ends of my whiskers. More white things landed. This time, on both sides of my whiskers. I watched as the little things turned—almost like magic—into drops of water.

One landed on my nose. It felt cold and made it wiggle. I stuck my tongue out.

It took a second, but finally a little silver-white speck landed on it. It felt cold.

"It's ice."

My tongue went back in my mouth.

It felt wet.

"No, it's water."

Very cautiously, Barkus eased up beside me.

"Well? What is it, ice or water?"

I caught some more of the stuff with my tongue.

"It's both," I answered.

"It can't be both," Barkus grumped. "Here, let me see."

He scooted up beside me and kind of shoved me over.

"Oh," he said gleefully, "it's snow."

"Snow?"

"Yes," he answered. "When I was just a tiny baby in the kennel with my mama, it snowed. I remember, now. Mama said that it usually didn't snow in June, but during the winter there would be lots and lots of it. It would even hide the grass. It's okay, though." He nudged me with his shoulder. "Snow won't hurt you."

I caught more of the funny, white "snow" on my tongue. I liked the way it felt. Barkus went back and piled up the towels with his front paws. I glanced over my shoulder at him.

"You're not scared anymore?"

He shook his head. "I just forgot what it sounded like." He smiled. "Now that I know what it is, I'm not scared. Snow is fun."

I fell asleep beside Barkus. The sound of the snow's gentle caress on our roof was better than a soft breeze rustling the trees. I slept like a baby curled up next to my friend.

Saturday morning, the white stuff was everywhere. It glistened and shimmered even more in the sunlight than it had last night.

As soon as Barkus got up, he went tearing out into it. He made a big circle around the yard and then came back inside.

"It's fun," he said. "Let's go play."

"Isn't it cold?"

I felt warm and cozy, nestled down in the towels. Barkus shrugged.

"It's a little cold at first," he admitted. "It feels funny because your feet sink into it. But, after a minute or two, it's not cold anymore, and it's fun."

I followed him to the door. There, I stopped and reached out a paw to touch the strange, white snow.

It *was* cold!

I yanked my paw back and sniffed at it. My paw smelled of water—only crisp, cold water. Barkus was right. It wasn't as cold as I thought.

I didn't sink in it like he told me I would. I guess it was because my feet were wider and I wasn't as heavy as Barkus. His feet sunk in, almost clear to the ground. My paws only dented the snow a little.

I had just started to explore this new, white world, when the back door burst open and Timmy and Jessica came tearing out. They'd just barely jumped from the step when I heard the mama calling behind them.

"You two get back in here," she yelled. "You get

your coats and your boots on before you go play in the snow."

Grumbling to themselves, they went back inside.

I had explored most of the backyard and was just about to climb the fence when I heard my Jessica call me.

We ran and played and wrestled and tumbled in the soft, white powder.

Barkus was right. Snow was fun to play in. In fact, I was having so much fun that I didn't even notice how close our play had taken us to the cellar. I didn't even think about it—not until the smell caught my nose.

It was the *fresh* smell of rat.

Chapter 9

The smell terrified me. My claws sprang out. Every muscle tensed. I began struggling to get away.

Somehow, I managed to catch myself. My Jessica was holding me. "Don't ever scratch or bite your special person," my mama had told me. My claw was almost touching her hand when I remembered.

It took every ounce of strength for me to pull my claws back in. My fur began to smooth down.

Timmy took hold of the handle on the door to the cellar.

"This is going to make a great playhouse," he said.

"Yeah," my Jessica agreed. "When it gets real cold this winter, we can come here and play with Barkus and Mewkiss."

Timmy made a grunting sound when he pulled on the door. "Bet the people who lived here before us left a mess down here, just like they did in the garage. It's probably going to take a lot of work to clean it up."

With her free hand, Jessica reached to help him lift the door.

"Yeah, but it's still going to be a great playhouse."

The snow slid off in a clump when they lifted the door and let it fall back on its hinges. The horrible smell of rat swept through the air. It wasn't an old smell. This odor was new! There were rats in the cellar!

Ten steps led into the dark, gaping hole. Timmy started down. Barkus was right beside him.

"No, Barkus!" I screamed. "Don't go!"

He didn't hear me.

I knew I'd never see my friend again. He and his Timmy disappeared into the dark hole. My Jessica started toward the opening.

It was like someone had rammed a white-hot stick into my back. At the same instant my insides went cold as ice. I don't know what happened when the panic took hold of me. I can't remember.

One moment, my Jessica was carrying me toward the steps that led into the cellar. The next, I was hiding in our doghouse, trembling. My Jessica was sobbing as she held her hand and ran toward the house.

"Mama, Mama," she cried, "Mewkiss scratched me."

The shame was almost more than I could stand. I had done a terrible thing and I felt so awful, I didn't know if I could ever show my face outside the dog-house again. I tried to bury myself in the towels. I curled up in a tight ball and hid my head with my tail. As bad as I felt for having scratched my Jessica, I guess I would have spent the rest of my life right there—if it hadn't been for Barkus.

He grabbed my tail.

My insides felt so bad, I didn't even notice the pain. He tugged harder.

"Come on, Mewkiss. You've been in here all day. Let's go play."

I only lay there.

He chomped down harder. Then he let go and coughed. I guess he got some of my hair in his mouth.

"Jessica's all right," he told me. "You didn't mean to scratch her, and she knows it. Now, quit feeling sorry for yourself and come on."

I flopped my tail back over my head to hide my face.

"I mean it," he said. "You can't spend the rest of your life in here. Come on."

I buried myself deeper in the pile of towels.

"No. Leave me alone."

"Are you scared of the rats?"

"No," I lied, shivering.

He nudged me with his nose. "Well, if you are, you don't need to be. They're gone. As soon as Timmy and I went down the steps, they took off."

I just lay there.

"You know that pile of bricks?"

I didn't answer.

"Well," he went on, "it goes clear down to the bottom of that cellar room. When they saw us coming, they climbed up through the opening. They were clamoring all over each other. Screaming and squeaking, like they were scared to death. I went to chase them, but they were so scared, they were clear past the fence before I could even get up the steps. I bet they're still running. Now, come on. Play with me. Please."

When I didn't move or answer, he was quiet for a moment. I heard him sigh as he plopped down on his haunches. For a long time, he sat there. Finally, I heard him snicker.

"All right," he whispered, "you asked for it."

Barkus bit down on my tail again. He lifted it off

my face. I glanced up and saw him holding it in his mouth as he looked at me with his soft, brown eyes. Then, instead of chewing on it, he started tugging.

"If you're not going to come out by yourself, I'll drag you out by your tail."

He growled and shook his head and began pulling. Frantic, I started grabbing and clawing for anything I could get hold of. It was no use. I could feel myself slide across the floor. In desperation, I clawed at the pile of towels. Barkus kept tugging on my tail. Now the towels and me, both, were sliding toward the door.

At the opening, I managed to grab the sides with my claws. I hung on for dear life.

"Let go," Barkus growled. He shook his head and leaned back, pulling for all he was worth.

I pulled, trying to get back into the house. Barkus pulled, trying to drag me out. I pulled. He pulled. Back and forth, back and forth. It was like a tug-of-war game, with my tail as the rope.

At last, it dawned on me that I either had to let go, or Barkus was going to yank my tail out—by the roots.

I released my hold on the doorway and spun around. My claws barely missed his soft nose. He gave my tail one last tug, then let go and sat down on his haunches.

"Quit being such a coward," he scolded. "When we play-fight, you're always telling me how rough and tough you are. Quit acting like such a baby."

A red puff of smoke exploded before my eyes. My teeth clamped together so tight that inside my head, it sounded like I had gravel in my mouth.

"Don't call me a baby," I snarled, laying my ears flat against my head. "And I am *not* a coward, either."

"You sure act like a coward," he scoffed.

I'd never been so mad at anyone or anything before. In a flash, I tore into him. My claws slashed at him, my teeth lashed out, grabbing at anything I could get hold of.

My attack surprised me as much as it did Barkus.

Within seconds, he fought back. I was quicker, but he was heavier and stronger. He bit down hard on one of my paws. I scratched his ear, and he let go. Then his sharp teeth tore into the soft flesh under my arm.

I hissed and snarled. Barkus growled and snapped. We rolled and tumbled across the yard. Our fur flew and the sounds of our battle shook the crisp, morning air.

It was a fight to the death.

Chapter 10

I guess we really might have hurt each other, if it hadn't been for the mama.

It wasn't a "play fight." It was as real as any fight could be. We squalled and yowled and bit and clawed. And suddenly, in the midst of all our racket, there was a loud WHOMP.

Something hit me right on the head. Then, there was another WHOMP. This time, whatever it was hit Barkus. His painful hold on my hind leg loosened.

Still biting at each other, we glanced up.

The mama stood above us. She had a rolled-up newspaper in her hand. She brought it down again, then again.

"Quit that!" she screamed as she pounded us with the paper. "You two stop. Quit!"

Barkus let go. He tucked in his tail and went whimpering into the doghouse. I ran over to the fence and squeezed through the crack. I scampered up the tree at the side of Allergies's yard.

I climbed out on a limb and rested there, panting. The fight took a lot out of me. It was a mean fight. But the mama beating us with the newspaper—that almost scared me to death.

Slowly I felt my fur unfuzz. The limb was wide so I sat down and began licking my wounds. My leg and my paw hurt where Barkus had bit me. I cleaned the wound and tried to make the hurt go away.

"You get in a fight?"

The voice startled me. I jumped and almost fell off my perch. I caught myself and looked around. Allergies was curled up on his back porch. He was close to the house and nestled in a spot that was dry and not covered with snow.

"You startled me," I said. "I didn't see you there."

"Sorry," he sniffed. "Fast as you went tearing up my tree, it's little wonder you didn't see me."

He lay his head down on his paws and watched me out of one eye.

"You hurt?"

I licked my leg again.

"Not bad."

He sniffled and rubbed his nose with a paw. "What was the fight about?"

My ears lay back against my head.

"My best friend called me a coward," I snarled. "There are rats in our cellar."

"Yes, I know," Allergies said. "In the summer, they live far out in the woods. But when winter comes, they move to the old cellar to raise their family. They've lived there for two years, now."

"But my Jessica and her brother are going to make a playhouse in the cellar. They want to play down there."

"That's bad," Allergies wheezed. "Children shouldn't play around rats." He looked up at me and coughed. "And when the children tried to take you down into the cellar, you ran away?"

"Yes," I admitted. "But I'm not a coward."

Allergies raised an eyebrow.

"Then why did you run away?"

"I'm a kitten," I sniffed. "My mama told me that when I was a grown cat, I would be brave and strong." I rubbed a paw across my eye, hoping Allergies hadn't seen the tear that squeezed out. "But . . . but," I stammered, "with a name like Mewkiss . . . I don't know if I'll ever be brave."

Suddenly, the hair on my back raised to a ridge. "But I'm not a coward. I'm not!"

Allergies didn't say any more. He only sniffled again and closed his eyes. I got to my feet and started clawing the tree, sharpening my claws.

I'm not a coward, I repeated to myself. I'm not. I'm not. I'm not!

I stayed in the tree almost the entire day. In the late afternoon, Allergies went inside when his special person called him. As his tail was disappearing through the door, I heard him call:

"Don't spend too long in my tree, Mewkiss. It's going to be a cold night."

When it got dark, I went back to our doghouse. Barkus looked up when I came in, but he didn't say anything. Neither did I.

We slept, that night, in opposite corners of our home.

The next two weeks, we slept in opposite corners. The snow had melted the day after our big fight, so it wasn't as cold. Still, the nights were chilly and it would have felt good to snuggle against someone.

We didn't, though.

Two or three days after our big fight, we apologized to each other. Barkus said he was sorry for calling me a coward and biting me. I told him I was sorry for biting his leg and leaving the big scar above his eye from my claws.

But we didn't play-fight. We didn't talk much, either. And at night, we slept apart.

During those two weeks, Timmy and Jessica came home almost every day from school and went straight to the cellar. They took brooms and trash cans down with them. They brought up cardboard boxes full of paper and trash. They carried out two, big, wooden boxes full of apple cores and old, rusty cans of fruits and vegetables.

Every day, when Jessica got home, she would call for me. I hid in the tree behind Allergies's house until she and Timmy were through working on their playhouse in the cellar.

Only then would I come and play with my special person.

My paw and my leg quit hurting—but my insides still felt bad. So each day, when Barkus was taking his afternoon nap, I'd sneak out of the doghouse and walk toward the cellar. Every day, I managed to get a little bit closer before I started to shake and the fear would make the hair on my back prickle up.

Each time I went toward the cellar, I would sniff the air. There was no odor of fresh rats.

I prayed that they were gone forever.

Chapter 11

My courage grew with each passing day. One afternoon, I had gone clear to the cellar. I had touched the shiny, metal door with my paw. I hadn't run away.

I curled up on my side of our doghouse. From behind me, I could hear Barkus snoring. I curled my tail around to cover my face and peeked over it.

I felt strong and brave inside.

Tomorrow, I told myself. Tomorrow, I will stand on top of the cellar. I will go clear to the bricks where I first smelled the rats. I *won't* run away.

Sleep that night was more peaceful than I could ever remember. I felt better about myself. I knew I would make myself become a strong, fearless, brave cat.

*   *   *

I woke in the middle of the night with Barkus's paw draped across my face. He still smelled like a dog, but it was the first time we had touched in almost two weeks. I didn't move away from him.

When I looked around, I figured out how we'd gotten together. The snow was falling and it was very cold. Somehow, we had both worked our way to a corner of the doghouse to get warm.

It felt good to sleep with my best friend close to me again.

But in the morning he was gone.

When I realized Barkus wasn't beside me, I woke with a start. I raised my head and looked all around. He wasn't in the doghouse. The snow that had fallen during the night was deep. A wall of white covered half the doorway to our house. Still barely awake, I stood up and peered over the wall of snow.

I could see the tracks Barkus had left in the snow. My eyes followed them. Finally, I saw my friend. He was far out in the yard. He stood close to the mound of dirt, staring at the pile of bricks with the hole that led to the cellar.

I felt uneasy as I watched him. Barkus didn't move. He didn't wiggle his stub tail. He didn't blink. I couldn't even see him breathing. It was like he was frozen—his eyes fixed on the hole in the brick.

I knew the rats were back.

Somehow, I managed to climb over the wall of snow. I walked toward my friend. I walked toward the cellar where the rats were.

I was almost to the mound of dirt when Barkus's eyes moved. He shot me a quick glance, then turned back to the bricks.

I could tell from his look that he was listening to something. He warned me, with that glance, to be very, very quiet.

There's nothing as quiet as cat feet in the snow. I stepped so cautiously and softly that the silvery-white crystals didn't even crunch beneath my paws. Moving forward took all the courage I had. But, finally, I was beside him—looking at the hole in the brick.

I smelled the rats. I heard their scratching.

But I didn't run away.

Then I could hear their voices.

"We must," one said.

"It's too dangerous," the other answered. "The big people might get us."

There was more scratching.

"This is our home. If the people children keep playing here, they'll destroy our food stash. I can't

have my babies with them around. They'll find them and kill our children. We *have to* get rid of them."

"But if we do what you suggest," the other ratty voice argued, "the big people may come and try to kill us. They may set traps or try to feed us poison."

"No, no," the wife answered, "they won't kill us. They might use traps or poison. But we know of those things. We won't be fooled. Those children play here most every day. We have to get rid of them."

I glanced at Barkus. His eyes were tight. His lip curled to a snarl, but he didn't make a sound.

"I don't like it," said one of the rats. "It's very dangerous."

"It is the only way. We will hide beside the steps. When they come to play, we must move quickly. The girl-child would be best. She is not quite as fast or strong as the boy-child. As soon as her foot leaves the last step, the one of us who is closest must leap and bite her on the leg. We must bite hard and make it hurt. Then we will run away and hide in the woods until the big people are through searching for us. When we return, the people children will not come back. After we bite the girl, they will not bother us again."

My eyes grew wide. I glanced over at Barkus. His

white, shiny teeth glistened like the snow. Then he growled.

"Shush," a ratty voice whispered from the hole in the bricks, "I thought I heard something."

My legs started to shake. My tail started to puff up like a balloon. I wanted to run, but I couldn't. I was frozen in the snow. I stood like a stone statue.

From below, I could hear whispering, but I couldn't hear what the rats were saying.

Then in a very loud voice, one said, "I smell something."

"Yes," the other agreed, "I smell puppy."

"And kitten, too," the other said.

Suddenly, a sharp nose appeared at the hole. Ratty whiskers wiggled.

I couldn't breathe. I couldn't blink. I could only stand there—frozen. Barkus snarled.

A second pointy noise appeared at the hole. Its whiskers wiggled, too.

"A fat, juicy puppy and a fat, juicy kitten would taste very good. They would make a nice meal. I'm hungry. Let's eat them!"

Barkus and I ran!

Chapter 12

About halfway across the yard, Barkus stopped. He wheeled around and started barking. He snarled and growled and barked as loud as he could.

I never looked back. I could feel the snow flying up as I charged across the yard. A long ways from the back door, I made a flying leap. I had never jumped so hard or so far before. But I landed in the center of the screen door.

I hit so hard, the air was almost knocked out of me. It made a terrible noise. I clung tight with my claws. I started shaking the door, making all the noise that I could.

Barkus barked, I meowed—as loud and hard and fast as I could. I rubbed my whiskers against the screen door.

I tried to live up to my name.

Not that it did any good.

The daddy finally opened the wooden door.

"Rats!" I meowed at the top of my voice. "Rats in the cellar. They're going to eat Barkus and me. They're going to bite Jessica."

The daddy just gave me a funny look and shook his head.

"This cat's getting plum crazy," he told the mama. "Think we need to take him to the vet and get him fixed?"

"No," I meowed, "I don't need fixed. I need help!!!"

Then he looked past me at Barkus.

"Dog's getting nutty as a fruitcake, too," he told the mama. Then he pushed open the screen. "Shut up, you dumb mutt. You're going to wake the whole neighborhood."

Barkus barked. I meowed.

It didn't do any good. The daddy slammed the screen. I watched as he pulled his rubber boots on over his socks and pajama legs.

When he started back toward the door, I leaped from the screen. I just barely managed to get out of the way before he flung open the door and stomped out into the snow.

Once the daddy came out, the two ratty noses

and ratty whiskers disappeared down the hole. Barkus kept barking. The daddy reached down and picked him up. He looked all around, like he was trying to see what Barkus was barking at. But when he didn't see anything, he marched back toward the house and threw Barkus into the garage. Then he slammed the door.

As the daddy started toward the door, I realized that once he was inside, I'd be all alone. Just me and the rats.

The mama saw him coming and opened the door for him.

In the blink of an eye, I charged through the opening. She tried to shove me back, but I was too quick for her. I leaped over her foot and raced for my Jessica's room.

I flew up the stairs like a streak of lightning. She wasn't there. I raced back downstairs. The sound of the TV took me to the living room. Timmy and my Jessica were curled up on the couch, watching Saturday-morning cartoons.

I leaped to the back of the couch, then jumped down and landed on her stomach.

"Rats," I meowed, "rats in the cellar. They're going to bite you."

She patted my head.

I moved up beside her. "Rats," I meowed. Then

I kissed her with my whiskers. "Rats," I mewed. Then, I kissed her again. Mew then Kiss. Mew. Kiss. Mewkiss.

My Jessica didn't understand. She pushed me back, then held me tight in her arms and rubbed my fur.

"I love you, too," she said. "As soon as the cartoons are over, we'll come and play."

"No," I cried, "you must understand! You've got to listen . . ."

The mama picked me up by the back of my neck. When she looked at me, her lip kind of curled up on one side.

"I think I'll call the vet. There's definitely something wrong with this crazy cat." Then—she threw me outside.

Frantically, I scratched at the door. They wouldn't let me back in. I ran to the garage.

From inside, I could hear Barkus scratching. I put my nose down to the crack under the door.

"Barkus!" I pleaded. "What do I do? Help me!"

I felt his breath when he put his nose down at the crack.

"I can't get out." He sniffed. "You have to stop the rats. You can't let them bite my Timmy or your Jessica. You've got to stop them."

"But how?" I wiped the tear from my whisker. "What can I do?"

Suddenly, there was a noise behind me. I looked back. The head of a rat appeared at the hole in the bricks. The rat smiled and licked his lips.

Chapter 13

I watched from the limb in the big tree in Allergies's backyard.

I watched when Timmy and my Jessica came and got shovels from the garage. I watched Barkus go flying out and start barking at the cellar. I watched when the daddy came out and got him, told him to "Shut up," then locked him back in the garage. I watched when Allergies came out the back door and limped out in his yard to use the bathroom. I watched how stiff and old he was, and I felt sorry for him.

And, I watched as Timmy and my Jessica started clearing a path in the snow with their shovels. I watched them dig closer and closer to the cellar.

I had never felt so helpless. So scared.

How long I watched, I don't know. I do know that little drops of water squeezed from my eyes. They rolled down my fur to my whiskers. At the very tip, they stopped, freezing into tiny icicles that hung, glistening in the sun.

Timmy and Jessica dug and dug. At first the snow flew from their path in great, white-powdered clumps. As they shoveled farther into the yard, the snow didn't fly as far. Still, I could tell that in no time at all they would be at the cellar door. Once they had the snow cleared from it . . .

My Jessica . . . those nasty rats . . .

I shuddered at the thought.

One of the tear icicles fell from the tip of a whisker.

"Hey," a grumpy voice called, "what are you doing up my tree?"

Allergies stood at the bottom of the tree looking up at me. When I didn't answer, he made kind of a wheezing sound and hobbled back toward his porch.

Then it hit me. Allergies was a cat. Sure, he was old and weak and sickly—but he was still a cat.

I shimmied down the tree and raced toward him. When he heard me coming, he turned to look. His head moved slowly and in little jerks, like it hurt him to look around.

"Allergies. Allergies," I pleaded, "you've got to

help me. The rats are going to bite my Jessica. Barkus and I heard them talking. Please come. Please help me."

Allergies didn't stop. He just kept walking toward his back porch. "I'm too old to be chasing rats," he said. "In fact, I'm gonna do good to make it back to my porch."

I walked beside him. His walk was as shaky as somebody who got stuck in a paint mixer—one slow, trembling step at a time.

"You've got to help me," I begged. "Barkus is locked in the garage. I can't do it alone. Please help. Please come."

He stopped. Without turning his head, he looked at me out of the corner of his eye.

"You're kidding," he said. "Look at me. I'm so old my bones creak when I walk. My arthritis is so bad I can barely get across my own yard. And you want me to come chase rats? Forget it!"

"But . . . but . . ."

He toddled on his way. I sat down in the snow and began to meow loudly. Timmy and Jessica were almost to the cellar. Allergies had been my last hope.

I watched him walking away from me. He wobbled as he walked. Each step seemed to hurt.

Maybe he was right. He couldn't help me. There was no one to help. I was all alone.

It took him forever to climb his way up the three steps to his back porch. Once there, he sat down on his bony, old hips and turned to look out in his yard.

"Besides," Allergies said in a weak, shaky voice, "with a name like yours—you don't need any help."

I frowned, tilting my head to the side.

"Huh?"

Allergies leaned against the door, trying to take some of his weight off his sore legs.

"Your name," he repeated. "If you'd just try to live up to your name—well, shoot—that name's enough to take on a dozen rats."

Quickly, I trotted over to him. I sat down on the step and looked him square in the eye.

"My name?" I wondered aloud. "I *did* live up to my name. I jumped on the screen and mewed. I kissed it with my whiskers. When I got inside, I ran straight to my Jessica. I mewed. I kissed her. What more can I do? I did what my name is—Mewkiss."

Allergies laughed.

I wanted to curl up and die. Here I was, begging for him to help me save my Jessica—and all he could do was laugh at me. I leaned my nose closer and glared at him. I hoped he could feel the daggers

coming from my eyes. I hoped he could feel the pain of my look, clear down in his old stiff joints.

He only laughed at me again.

"Never seen such a dumb cat," he said with a chuckle. He snickered so hard, it made him cough. "You got your name all screwed up. That's all that's wrong."

I cocked my head. My tail flipped.

"What do you mean?"

"Mewkiss," he chuckled again. "You think your name is Mew and Kiss stuck together. You dumb old kitten. It's Mukiz, that's spelled M-u-k-i-z. It's pronounced almost the same way—little more of a 'z' sound at the end, and not so much 'hiss'—but there's all the difference in the world between Mewkiss and Mukiz. Didn't your mother ever tell you about him?"

My tail flipped impatiently. It jerked and twitched in all directions.

"What? Who?"

Allergies shook his head. "Mukiz. The greatest warrior of ancient Egypt. You never heard of him?"

I shook my head.

Allergies drew back. "Your mama didn't tell you about Mukiz?"

"No."

"I'll swear," he laughed. Then, he started cough-

ing and wheezing and had to stop so he could catch
his breath.

Behind me, I heard the sound of metal hitting
against metal. Timmy and Jessica were clearing the
snow from the cellar door.

"Tell me of Mukiz," I pleaded, turning to face
him again. "Please, Allergies. Tell me. Tell me. Was
he a brave Egyptian warrior?"

Allergies took a deep breath.

"No. Mukiz was a cat. According to legend, cats
were given the names of brave soldiers. Mukiz was
so brave and such a fierce fighter, the Egyptians
gave him his own name."

"Did he kill rats?" I pleaded desperately.

"Rats," Allergies scoffed. "Rats were nothing to
old Mukiz. He was so brave and strong, he could
take on a whole army of rats. He didn't bother with
piddly, ole rats. He used to fight soldiers."

"Soldiers?"

"Sure." He nodded. "The way the legend had it,
Mukiz used to ride on his special person's shoulder
when he went into battle. If someone tried to sneak
up and attack them from behind, Mukiz would leap
on them and rip them to shreds. Bravest fighter
who ever lived."

Behind me, I heard a CLUNK sound. Timmy put his shovel aside. Jessica reached for the handle on the cellar door. "Go on down to our playhouse," called Timmy, walking back toward the garage. "I'll go get Barkus so he can play with us."

Allergies put a shaky old paw on my shoulder.

I turned to face him. His eyes were solemn and deep as pools of liquid fire.

"With a name like yours," he smiled, "you don't even have to live up to it. All you have to do is *try*, and you can beat up a ton of rats."

Jessica opened the cellar door.

"Mukiz is the strongest, bravest, most powerful name a cat could ever hope for," he whispered. "And the name is all yours!"

Chapter 14

My Jessica's foot was on the bottom step, just as I reached the cellar door. There was no time to run down the stairs. Her foot was almost on the floor.

I jumped—clear from the top step to the bottom. In midair, I saw something move. I spun my tail, adjusting my leap.

Just as the rat lunged for my Jessica's leg, I slammed into it.

We went sprawling across the cement floor. Jessica squealed and yanked her foot back to the step. I leaped up and whirled around. The other rat was beside her, still hidden by the side of the cellar wall.

I charged.

The rat squeaked and ran behind a box.

I spun around. The rat I had slammed into struggled to its feet. He was the male. He was bigger than the one who snuck behind the box. He was almost as big as me.

Still dazed from my attack, he shook himself. I leaped. In the blink of an eye, he dodged. His fur puffed out, making him look even bigger than he was. He snarled, baring his sharp, ratty teeth.

"I'll kill you," he threatened. "You're just a kitten. I'll eat you up. I'll . . ."

My whole insides seemed to tumble. My heart pounded in my ears. He was huge. He wasn't half-grown, like me. This was an adult rat—with big muscles and sharp teeth and angry eyes.

I wanted nothing more than to climb the tree in Allergies's backyard. It was high up there. It was safe.

"I haven't eaten all day," he growled, down deep in his throat. He bared his white fangs, clear to the gums.

His teeth were like long daggers. His gums glistened pink and wet. Black, beady eyes burned into me like a hot fire. He took a step toward me.

"I'll fill my tummy with a fat, juicy kitten!"

My insides and my outsides—both—wanted to

run away and hide. Instead, I arched my back and hissed. Keeping myself between the rat and my Jessica, I moved toward him.

"My name is Mukiz," I spit. "No rat can face the fury of Mukiz."

I hissed again and stabbed at him with my claws. He leaped away, snapping with his sharp teeth. Slowly, one step at a time, he started to retreat.

Suddenly, I heard Barkus. He came yapping and thundering his way down the steps. "I'll save you, Mewkiss. I'm coming."

Still snarling and hissing, I turned to glance at him. "Get the one behind the box," I called. "I can handle this one."

Barkus raced over to the box. He sniffed around for a second, then started barking and digging, trying to get the other rat.

I had only glanced away for a second. When I looked back, my rat was almost to the opening under the bricks.

"Come back and face me, you coward," I screamed. I leaped and caught him with my claws, pulling him away from the hole.

Jessica screamed and ran from the cellar.

The rat's sharp, spike teeth clamped shut on my cheek. The taste of my own blood was salty and bittersweet. Somehow, I shook him loose. As he ran to the far side of the cellar, I clawed at him again. A claw stuck in his hip. He spun around.

Before I could let go, his sharp teeth jabbed my paw. I felt them sink in. I felt the crunch as teeth met bone.

Suddenly, I was scared. It hurt more than I imagined *anything* could. I wanted to run.

I didn't.

Bravely, I tried to yank my foot from his snarling grasp. His jaws ground shut. He wouldn't let go.

Then I saw his neck. Despite my pain—despite my fear—I pulled him toward me. My paw throbbed, but I drew it back, and along with it came the rat.

I took a deep breath and lunged. My teeth sank into the soft flesh at his throat. With my free paw, I clung to him. I balled up and started kicking with the claws of my hind feet.

He let go of his grip on my paw and tried to run. I hung on.

He was so big and strong that he dragged me across the concrete floor. I bit harder. I clawed and kicked and hissed—and bit down even harder.

We were almost to the opening that led up into the bricks when he fell. I never loosened my grip for a second. He fought and snapped at me. I bit harder.

Finally, it was over. He made a gurgling sound in his throat, then he was still.

The smell of death filled the room.

I still hung onto him. Suddenly, out of the corner of my eye, I saw the other rat come flying from behind the box. With Barkus hot on her heels, she made it to the hole and scurried up.

He was chasing her so fast, he ran smack into the brick wall. He shook his head, then spun and raced up the steps.

When I was sure my rat was dead, I picked him up in my mouth and climbed the stairs to see if Barkus needed help.

The rat was too quick for my friend. She had already squeezed through the fence before Barkus could get to her. He stood at the fence, barking his rage because he couldn't get through and catch her.

Just then, the back door flew open. Timmy, Jessica, the mama, and the daddy came flying across the yard. When they saw what I had in my mouth, they rushed up to me.

"He's got the rat," my Jessica boasted. "Mewkiss killed the rat. I told you there was a rat, Daddy. See?"

I laid the dead rat at my Jessica's feet.

It was only then that they noticed the blood that poured from my cheek and my foot. It didn't hurt, though. In fact, when my Jessica swooped me up in her arms and rushed me toward the house—it felt almost good. The wounds were deep, but they were proud wounds. Proud wounds that I had earned in battle.

Barkus caught up to us about halfway across the yard. He bounced and leaped against Jessica's leg, trying to see if I was all right.

"I'm fine," I told him.

"I missed the other rat," he said. "I'm sorry. She was too fast for me. You think she'll come back?"

I leaned around my Jessica's arm so I could see him.

"We'll never see that rat again," I answered. "Rats are cowards."

And I thought to myself, "But *I'm* not. Mukiz is no coward. I'm the bravest cat of all.

Chapter 15

By the time we got to the vet to get stitches put in my cheek and leg, I didn't feel quite so brave anymore. I mean, a doctor's office is a really scary place.

Then, I figured—here I am, still only a half-grown kitten. If I was brave enough to take on a big, mean rat . . . what're a couple of stitches?

It didn't hurt at all.

My people were real nice to me when I got home. I got to stay inside by the fireplace for three whole days. They burned wood logs in it and it made the whole room feel warm and cozy. They fed me, and my Jessica loved and petted me every chance she got. She even read to me. That was my favorite thing. I would lie across the back of her neck while she leaned on the cushion in her chair. The sound of her voice and just having her touch me—that was the best medicine in the world for my hurts.

When the mama finally let me go outside, Barkus was nice to me, too. He was excited to see me. He jumped up and down and ran in big, wide circles around me. But he knew my paw still hurt, so he didn't pull my tail or want to wrestle. He *did* want to know every little detail of what happened at the vet's.

His biggest and most important question was: "How come you were scared to death of rats, then all of a sudden, you managed to get so brave?"

I told him all about the legend of Mukiz—just like Allergies had told it to me. Barkus's eyes got as big as saucers when I told the story. I was proud of my name. I could tell that Barkus was proud *for* me. I knew by the way his chest puffed up and the way his little, stub tail wagged as he listened.

Then, while it was still light outside, I went to see Allergies. I wanted to thank him for telling me of my *real* name.

Only, Allergies wasn't outside.

In fact, I didn't see him for the next three weeks. Every day, I'd limp over to check his yard. I didn't climb the tree to look for him, because my paw was too weak for climbing. I *did* hobble all around the yard looking for him. I guess his special person kept him inside. It was very cold out and he was quite sickly.

After a week, my people took me back to the vet to get my stitches out. And after the second week, I felt well enough to go wrestle with Barkus. He even grabbed my tail a few times.

But, still no Allergies.

One day, about four weeks after the big fight with the rats, the sun came out. There was still a good two feet of snow on the ground. Today was a bright and gorgeous day, though. It was so warm that the water dripped from the long icicles on the roofs of the houses. I climbed up the big tree in Allergies's backyard. I no longer needed to hide there. But it was a tall tree and I could see a long ways. Besides, nestled on the bare branches, I could soak up the warm sunshine.

I was about to take a little catnap when I heard Allergies's special person open the door. Only this time, instead of letting him out, she laid him tenderly on the porch. She petted him and told him how much she loved him. I couldn't help notice the sad tone of her voice.

As soon as she went inside, I shuffled down the tree trunk and went to talk with him.

He didn't get up and hobble out into the yard, like he usually did.. He didn't move much at all, in fact. When I came up and said, "Hi," he could barely turn to face me.

"What's wrong?" I asked.

"I'm very sick," he wheezed. "My arthritis hurts. My nose is running and my insides are all eaten up with cancer."

I frowned and looked at him.

"What's that?"

"It's a disease that people and animals get sometimes."

"Is it serious?"

He nodded—ever so slowly.

"Does it hurt bad?"

"Yes," he whispered, "but it won't hurt much longer. This afternoon my special person is taking me to the vet. They're going to put me to sleep."

I frowned again.

"What does that mean?"

His smile was weak yet gentle.

"That means that they are going to help me die."

My tail jerked. Then it dropped weakly to the ground.

"Oh, no! How terrible." I leaped up on the porch

beside him. "Come with me. I'll hide you. You can
live with Barkus and me in our house."

Allergies smiled.

"It's not horrible," he sighed. "It's not horrible at
all. Sometimes, when the hurt and pain are so bad
. . . sometimes I look forward to going on a nice,
long sleep. I'm just lucky to have a special person
who loves me enough to let me go."

I sat beside him and nudged him with my paw.

"I don't want you to go away, Allergies. We were
just starting to be friends. I love you. I don't want
you to leave."

He gave a little shrug. It was so small and weak,
I could hardly see it.

"It's all right," he sniffed. "Besides, there's not
much we can do about it. I'm ready. I'm brave."

When he told me he was brave, it reminded me
of why I had come to talk with him in the first place.

"Thank you for telling me about my real name," I
said. "I want to do something special. There's no
way I can ever *really* thank you, enough—but I
want to try."

Allergies looked at me strangely. His eyes were
old and tired—yet, for an instant, they almost
seemed to twinkle.

"I'm glad my special person let me come outside,
one last time," he said, closing his eyes and resting

his head on his paws. "I've been meaning to tell you about that."

I moved to the step below him. I inched over so I could look him in the eye.

"Tell me about what?"

He blinked as I stood there, almost nose to nose with him.

"About the legend of Mukiz . . ." he answered. Then he closed his eyes again, almost like he was drifting off to a sound sleep.

"What about the legend?"

He didn't answer, so I nudged his nose with mine. It felt warm and dry, instead of cold and damp. When I touched him, his eyes opened. I saw that same twinkle.

"What about the legend?" I prodded once more.

Allergies flipped his tail.

"I lied."

My eyes popped wide. My whole insides jerked. "You lied?"

He shrugged his feeble shoulders.

"Yep. I lied. I made up the story about Mukiz. It was a pretty good story, though, wasn't it?"

"You mean my real name's not Mukiz?"

"Yep."

"You mean there really wasn't a famous cat named Mukiz who lived in Egypt and fought soldiers?"

"Yep."

"But . . . but . . ." I stammered. My tail flipped, out of control, from side to side.

His tired old head drooped back on his paws.

"You're blocking my sunlight," he complained.

My tail puffed up—big and round.

"You lied! You lied!" I yelped. My claws sprang out.

He flipped his tail. I leaned my head to the side so I could glare into his eyes.

"Why?"

"I had to," he answered flatly. "Those rats were going to hurt your special person. You had to stop them, but you were afraid that you couldn't. Only, you really could. You just didn't know it."

All of a sudden, I felt dizzy. I guess it was from panting so hard and fast. I folded my tail under me and sat down on it.

"I can't believe it. You mean there never was a Mukiz? Then . . . then . . . my real name is Mewkiss. Just plain, old Mewkiss—just a dumb, stupid name."

He cocked an eyebrow. "You think Mewkiss is bad? How'd you like to be stuck with a name like Allergies?"

I sank down and lay my head on my paws. "I'm just Mewkiss," I sighed. "I'm not brave or strong.

All I can do is Mew and Kiss. I'm not special at all."

Suddenly, Allergies raised his head, faster than I had seen him raise it in months. Then, a big paw shot out. He boxed me square between my ears. I blinked and drew back. His eyes were stern.

"You *are* special," he hissed. "All of us are. Our names are important, but not nearly as important as what we have inside—what we *believe*."

He cocked an eyebrow.

"Were you scared when you fought the rat?"

"No!" I answered bravely.

Only, as soon as I said it, my whiskers started to twitch.

"Well, not really," I said.

Allergies coughed and just looked at me.

"Okay. So . . . well . . . when I saw how big the rat was . . . I guess . . . and when he bit my paw . . . maybe a little . . . and . . ." Suddenly, my tail began to twitch. I sighed. "Okay, so I guess I was a little scared. I guess I sort of wanted to run away."

"But you didn't?"

"No."

"You fought the rat even though you were scared?"

"Yes."

His look made me feel a little dumb. Then he gave a little shake of his old, wobbly head.

"That's all there is to being brave. Courage doesn't mean you're not scared. If you're brave, you go ahead and do the things you have to, even when you *are* scared. Your courage was there—inside of you—all along. You just didn't know it.

"You believed you were a coward. So you were. I made up a dumb story, and suddenly you believed you were brave and strong. So you were.

"Your name didn't make the difference when you fought that rat. What you believed—did!"

His stern eyes seemed to soften. His old head sank toward his paws. "I've found," he said softly, "if you believe in yourself, you can do most anything."

He winked at me and almost seemed to smile. Slowly, his old eyes began to close. His wobbly, heavy head drooped to his paws.

I didn't bother him anymore. But I stayed beside him until his special person came and carried him into the house.

I knew that I'd never see him again.

That night, I couldn't sleep. I felt awfully sad and empty inside. Barkus kept asking me what was wrong, but I couldn't talk about it. Finally, he curled up in the towels.

I lay, looking out the doorway at the moon for a

long, long time. It was a bright, full moon. It made the silvery flakes of snow glisten and shine like the little rocks in the mama's ring. I cried a little. The moonlight made the tiny, silvery crystals of ice on the tips of my whiskers shine, too.

"Are you all right?" Barkus asked from behind me.

I didn't answer.

He picked my tail up, gently, in his mouth.

"Maybe you'd feel better if we play. You want to play with me, Mukiz?"

Suddenly, my whiskers wiggled. The little, icicle tears fell off and fluttered to the floor.

"My name's not Mukiz," I boasted, "it's Mewkiss."

I lay my ears flat against my head—looking very mean, when I turned on him. Then, with a flip of my tail, I yanked it out of his mouth.

When I started swishing my tail back and forth and teasing Barkus with it, I knew what was going to happen next.

"And you best not pull my tail," I teased. "Because Mewkiss is the roughest, toughest, bravest cat in all the world!"